D1543986

PRE-SCHOOL
STORYBOOK

©1983 Schwager & Steinlein
English text ©Autumn Publishing.
English Language Edition, designed and
produced by Autumn Publishing Limited.

Published in Great Britain by Brown Watson (Leicester) Ltd.,
55A London Road, Leicester LE2 0PE.

ISBN 0 7097 0591 3

Printed in Czechoslovakia
50047

PRE-SCHOOL STORYBOOK

Brown Watson

ENGLAND

Contents

Going to the countryside

Sarah, Nick and Peter were getting ready to go on a journey. Nick packed his pullover. Sarah brought out blouses and dresses. The suitcase was already half full, and the boots still had to go in.

"I'm taking my wooden cow with me!" shouted Peter.

"Don't be silly!" said Nick. "There are plenty of cows where we're going!"

Sarah, Nick and Peter had loaded their baggage onto their toy motor car and they were whizzing through fields and tracks. The teddy-bear and doll were allowed to go, too. Nick blew the trumpet—Tati-tata! Make way!

"Watch out in front," said Sarah to Peter, "otherwise you'll hit the fence."

But Peter had already pressed the brake pedal down and stopped the car. The others shouted, "Go on further."

"No," said Peter, "look at that field full of cows and sheep. Let's have a closer look at them."

The children lived in a town and knew about dogs and cats, guinea pigs and hamsters, canaries and budgies. But some animals they only knew about from looking at books, or the television. They got out of the car and went to the fence. Peter held out a handful of grass which he had plucked and two nosey cows came over

and ate the grass from Peter's hand. They looked
dangerous with their horns and large rosy muz-
zles. They chewed from side to side without
stopping. But they did not try to bite or kick the
children. The cows' tails swung all the time to
chase the flies away. The udders were full of

11

milk. Some of the cows were mooing loudly and a little while later the farmer came to milk them. The farmer skimmed the milk and from the cream which he had skimmed, he made butter, cream and cheese.

Nick fed a sheep, and Sarah held a tiny lamb

on her lap.

"I like sheep more than cows," said Sarah, "you can cuddle them, and you can knit gloves and pullovers with their wool."

"And they give milk and cheese too," said Nick, "and besides, they don't have horns."

Peter said, "Think again, Nick, do they really give us milk and cheese? They don't give us anything at all. We take their milk without asking them, and we have to make the cheese ourselves from milk!"

"Tell me," Sarah asked, "where do the holes in the cheese come from?"

Suddenly there was a "miaow..." from somewhere. Peter was pleased because he didn't know the answer to Sarah's question.

Sarah put the little lamb back on the grass and looked around the field in the direction of the sound. She discovered a mother cat with five kittens. Quietly, Peter and Nick crept closer. They wanted to hold the kittens but the mother cat protected her little ones and wanted them back. The children saw a mother fox under the pine trees, and the rabbit family behind the big stones. The deer was with her fawn, and the cow with her small calf. Everywhere in nature, the parents protect their young ones and watch over them with great care. When the ducks took their ducklings to the pond, mother duck went first and the baby ducks followed her to the water, walking in single file. The father duck watched from far away, and if danger threatened, he chased it away by flapping his wings. The mother fox was watching the ducks from her hideout, and wondered whether she should catch one. Her five little cubs were always hungry. A duckling would make a lovely meal for them. But she had already caught some fish from the pond, and now she was feeling lazy and satisfied. She let the ducks swim in peace. The father fox was hunting in the woods and mother fox must not leave the baby foxes alone. If they ran away into the meadow a bird of prey might have come and carried them away in its claws. That is how things are in nature. Danger

lurks everywhere for the baby foxes, too.

"Yes, puss," said Sarah to the mother cat, "here are your babies back again, they're so sweet. But do take good care of them."

Sarah, Nick and Peter carried on with their walk. They took off their shoes and socks and had a paddle in the stream which runs near the

farmhouse. They had stayed at the farmhouse last year so they knew the farmer very well. The children were really happy that they could stay with him for four weeks this year. They have such fun in the country and it was so different for them, as they lived in the town and didn't see all these animals there.

The farmer was hay-making and they went over to help him. They had learned all about raking the grass and building up the haystacks on their holiday last year. They didn't find a mouse last year though! The ginger cat tried to catch the mouse first.

All three children fell asleep feeling very tired and happy. The farmer hitched the toy car and suitcases to his tractor, and brought them to the farmhouse. He knew that the children were so busy enjoying themselves that they forgot to bring their belongings to the house.

At the garden centre

Each year when the snow has melted and the gardens become green again, Sarah, Nick and Peter visit Mr. Snail, the gardener.

The gardener doesn't find his name nice at all, because he doesn't like snails. They eat up all

his young plants, and he is always watching out for them. But although he sprays the ground and the leaves to make the snails lose their appetite, they are so crafty that they always find something to eat.

As Sarah, Nick and Peter walked to the nursery, they did exactly what Mr. Snail the gardener did. They looked to the right, then to the left then they picked up all the snails they could find. They put them in the wheelbarrow which Nick brought along to fill up with flowers and vegetables. Then they went to the next field and dumped the snails. They could nibble in this field to their heart's content without causing damage.

He also put a tiny fieldmouse in his barrow. Fieldmice nibble plants from underneath. They eat up all the roots, and the flowers then wilt away and die. Nick was pleased that he managed to catch a fieldmouse.

But Peter said to Nick, "We shouldn't catch mice, because if we take them from the nursery and put them in the field behind, they'll all be back here to-morrow."

"Be quiet a minute!" Nick whispered. "There are three little mice and the big grey cat is crouching in the bushes." Sarah saw a little mouse hiding in the wheelbarrow.

Peter said, "Come on, let's go. Don't disturb the cat if it wants to catch mice."

"It won't catch my mouse," Nick said, and drove it off to the field.

As the children looked out for the flowers they wanted to buy for Mummy, they saw the hot-houses. The roofs were all made of glass so that the sun can shine in from all sides. Inside them, the gardener sows tiny seeds into warm, damp earth. He watches out for the first green seed-lings to come out.

When the small seedlings become strong and
big, the gardener plants them in a garden bed
outside. Sarah, Nick and Peter wanted to help
him. They turned the earth with the spade, level-
led it with the small rake, so that the tender roots
could spread out freely. All the young flowers
have to be well watered.

Sarah wanted to know what the gardener did with all the flowers.

"I sell them to flower shops and stores," said the gardener, "and I also sell them for birthdays and weddings. But some flowers are left to dry up so that the seeds can ripen and fall out. That way, you can sow new flowers, or use the seeds for other things, such as sunflower margarine, or poppy-seed bread rolls."

"Oh yes, I have had poppy-seed bread, it tastes best with honey," said Sarah. She heard the bees buzzing away between the flower blooms and saw the butterflies fluttering up and down. "I know that honey comes from bees," said Sarah, "because they collect nectar from the flowers. But what are the butterflies doing on them?"

"They stretch their long sucking tubes into the bottom of the flower petals to drink the sweet liquid. They become hungry and thirsty, just as we do."

"And when it's dark, where do the butterflies spend the night?"

"They sleep between the leaves, their wings folded up, and in the morning they climb up, stretch out their wings and let the sunshine warm them."

Nick and Peter were having fun with a snail which seemed to be quite happy on top of Nick's head. "Now, let's go over to the vegetable patch," the gardener said, "and get some carrots and cabbages for you."

"You may also pick as many strawberries as you like. And chase away any rabbits you see."

At first, Sarah, Nick and Peter didn't see any rabbits. But just as they were about to move on, three of them sprang up through the cabbage patch. As the children passed the shop, Nick

put a cabbage on the ground to make room in
the small barrow for some flower seed packets.
"Mummy didn't say anything about those,"
called Peter. "Put the seeds back on the stall and
put the cabbage back in the barrow."

When they got back home the children put
the flowers in the vase and the plants in the plant

stands. They always made sure that the flowers had enough water. They gave the carrots and cabbage to Mummy and told her all about the animals and insects they had seen.

The animal park

When Sarah, Nick and Peter made a wish for a special trip, they asked if they could go to the animal park.

When they arrived, the animals they saw first were the rabbits and the hedgehogs. Whole

families of them went across the pathways and through the meadows.

Nick asked, "Can't we take a few hedgehogs or a small rabbit with us?"

"No, we may not." said Sarah. "They are too young now, and they need their parents. You can only take them home if you find them around in the winter."

"Be really quiet!" said Nick. "I know for sure that there are squirrels here!"

Peter discovered that a baby deer was standing near him. It was eating some leaves, very quietly. Sarah put her hand in front of her mouth. She was afraid to cough or make a noise to frighten the deer. Quite near her were a stag, another baby deer and a doe, a mummy deer.

Peter whispered, "I know why they are not running away. Daddy once said that when the wind blows from where the deer are standing, they don't smell people and are not afraid of them, even if they see them."

"That's right," said Sarah, "I remember this. When the hunter wants to know where the wind

is coming from, he wets one finger and holds it up in the air. The finger will be cold on the side where the wind blows. The hunter then knows how near he can go to the animals without them running off."

"I know something too," said Nick. "If you touch a baby deer, the smell of people stays on it. The other deer don't like that deer any more.

Then it will be lonely and may become ill and perhaps die."

"That's terrible," Sarah said. "Come on, let's move on." The three walked on into the woods, very carefully.

"What, rabbits again?" they cried out. "There's

a lot of them here!"

They all looked over the fence. At first they thought that all rabbits were alike. But when they looked more closely, they saw this was not so. Nick shouted, "I can see an Easter rabbit!"

"That's not possible," said Peter. "Easter rabbits are made out of marzipan or chocolate."

The children heard loud breathing. They also saw another fence. But they had no idea what animals were kept there. For a long while they stared at some low bushes. But they couldn't see anything.

Then they moved round to another tree, and they noticed in front of them that the whole tangle of plants was moving backwards and forwards. It was a badger. Its head was striped and he crept through the grass. The badger groped about like a small bear and moved all the shrubs in front of him. Nick whispered, "Look at that!" and showed the others where the badger was. "There's another one! Do you think they're both going hunting now?"

Peter answered, "No, they hunt at night. If they

come out in daytime, it's only to lie in the sun."

"And what do badgers eat?" asked Nick.

"Practically everything," answered Peter, "mice, roots, snails, small rabbits, beech-nuts. They eat what they can find."

"Has the badger got any enemies?" Nick wanted to know. "Is it afraid of the fox?"

"No, not at all," Peter answered, "sometimes it even lives together with the fox."

Reddish-brown shadows rushed up the tree. The branches crackled above Sarah, Nick and Peter. The squirrels were there! Of course, they were not behind a fence like the rabbits, the whole forest belongs to them!

Nick said, "Now they can have the nuts we brought with us." He opened his small bag, got the nuts out of it and put them down on the ground.

A squirrel climbed down the tree, picked up a nut, ran up the tree again and looked for a comfortable spot to eat. With its sharp teeth it soon opened the hard shell and dropped it so as to gnaw at the sweet nut kernel. The other

squirrels also came down and carried off the nuts lying on the ground. "I think they've got a really good hideout in this tree," said Peter.

"At last we now know where they live," Nick whispered.

But Sarah knew better, "A squirrel doesn't have just one place to live, it has two or three.

It plays in one of them, stores its food in the other, and then has another place where it can keep nice and warm when it snows."

"That's a bit silly," said Nick, "if it snows and the provisions are in another hiding place, surely it can't find the way to them, it must go hungry."

"Don't worry", said Peter, "it doesn't go hungry. It never forgets where it laid up its store and will always find it again, even when the snow covers the ground."

"When the squirrel looks for its hiding places, it just has to be careful not to be caught by the fox."

"Ah," said Nick, "I hope it's always on the look-out! I can't stand foxes."

As the three went on further, Nick soon forgot what he had said.

"Oh look, how sweet!" he called out.

"Real little baby foxes!"

"Can you touch them?" asked Nick.

"You'll be surprised," said Sarah. "If you go

near them, they'll scamper off straight away."

"Psst!" said Peter, "can you hear something?"

There was a grunting, snorting and squeaking. The wild boars were making the noises. It was lucky that there were fences all around them. The boar's tusks looked dangerous. "Let's go home," said Peter.

The new house

Sarah, Nick and Peter have moved. Daddy has built a house in the country and today they are spending the first day there. The children are very happy to be able to move into a house in the country with Daddy and Mummy.

Daddy said, "You three, sit on the seesaw, then I'll take a photograph to remember this great day!"

For several months, the children had watched as the new house was being built. They could hardly believe it was now completed. They remembered a certain Sunday last year when Daddy said, "Come on, climb in the car, we're going out of town. I've got a surprise for you today."

"What sort of surprise?" asked the three of them, and their parents answered, "You just wait, you'll soon see it!"

They drove through woods and over field tracks and Daddy suddenly stopped in a stubble-field and called out, "All out! We're at home!"

How could that be? There was only a waste field and an apple tree without apples. Sarah at once thought of Hansel and Gretel, and began to cry. Father then took her up in his arms and explained it all. How he had bought the field and the apple tree, and that they would build a lovely home on it. The children would be able to sing and make a noise without the neighbours in the flat below knocking their ceiling with the broom

stick! And here was the house, quite finished, and they would sleep in it tonight for the first time.

When they woke up the next morning, they couldn't remember where they were at first. But then, they romped around with the pillows and jumped with pleasure. It didn't do much good to the crocodile under the bed. The higher Nick jumped on his bed, the more his mattress went down when he landed back on it. Each time the poor crocodile got a thump on its head from the bed springs.

"Come on, let's be quiet again." said Peter. "Daddy and Mummy might still want to sleep." They all agreed.

"I know what," Sarah said, "we'll play the guessing game!"

"O.K." shouted Nick, "I already know somebody, I'll start. Well, have a guess! Who have I hidden in the left-hand corner behind Sarah's bed?"

Peter asked, "Is it a man?"

"No."

"Is it a lady?"

"Yes."

"Has she got a dog?"

"Yes."

"Is the dog black and shaggy and never brushed?"

"Yes."

"Then it's Mrs. Chatter who always stood in front of her door and shouted, "Can't you climb down the stairs quietly!"

Peter imitated the old woman's voice. The children all laughed, but they knew it wasn't very nice to make fun of other people, and so they thought of something else to do.

They got dressed and ran out into the garden.
Some neighbouring houses had also been built
and they saw the other children playing in their
gardens. Sarah, Nick and Peter only had to look
over the next door garden to make new friends.

In the afternoon, Daddy pumped up the rub-
ber swimming pool and filled it with water. The

children could splash and throw water about as much as they wanted, without being scolded.

"Come over, all of you," Peter shouted to the neighbouring children. Naturally, they were delighted at the invitation.

There were fresh strawberries and banana milk shake for tea. Mummy spread a large cloth

on the lawn, with a cup, a small dish and a spoon for each person. Peter asked his guests, "Who wants some more? Just help yourselves, as much as you like."

Mummy took a photograph. Six happy children in a garden!

Next day the sky was very cloudy and it was raining. But the three didn't want to stay at home.

They took the large umbrella, and a couple of cushions to put on the cold, wet stones and sat outside in the garden, looking at a picture book.

"Do you know," Sarah said to Peter, "Now that we can go straight in the garden from the front door, we could have a kitten. Or maybe two, or one each. What d'you think?"

"Fine," said Peter. "But it'll catch mice and run away."

"It'll always come back here when it knows this is its home. It can have my doll's cot or a small basket with a soft blanket to lie on. And we'll give it milk to drink."

"What if it prefers to eat mice?" Nick asked.

"Then I'll catch some for it," said Nick. "Be quiet, I think there's one here already!"

The tufts of grass were moving, but the children couldn't see whether it was a mouse, or just the wind blowing.

"What shall we call the kitten, then?" asked Peter.

Sarah said, "I think Sally is a nice name."

"Oh yes," cried Nick, "Sally is really a cute name for a cat."

Then the children had to ask Mummy and Daddy.

"Agreed!" they said. "You can have a kitten. Go and have a look in the letter box to see if the newspaper has come yet." Mummy said. "Perhaps someone has advertised some kittens for sale."

Sarah, Nick and Peter ran off to fetch the paper. But no one was selling cats; only budgies and sheep dogs were advertised.

Daddy said, "I think there is a cat's home nearby. Let's go and find out."

"What is a cat's home?" Peter asked.

"It is a bit like an orphan home for cats," replied Daddy. "When you find cats without a home, you can take them along there so that they will be looked after and fed. But you can also go there and buy a cat."

"Are there kittens in the home?" asked Nick.

"There certainly are," said Daddy. "Let's look in the phone directory to find the address." They

found the address, but it was too far away to go there that day.

The day arrived when they could go to the cat's home. It was a very big place and there was miaowing everywhere. There were so many cats that the children didn't know how to begin to choose one. Most of them were big and fat. Others were very skinny.

Sarah sat down. Suddenly, she felt two little paws on her arm. It was a tabby kitten. It purred and wanted to jump on her lap. The children all agreed, "This must be Sally!"

They took the kitten home and showed her her basket. Sally climbed straight in and went to sleep. Next day the children showed Sally the garden and she was very happy there.

At playschool

Sarah, Nick and Peter go to the playschool. They can take a doll with them, or a puppet, or any

small toy. They take a small satchel each, with a sandwich to eat at break-time. On the way to playschool they notice many things and talk about what they've seen. Some kittens pinched Nick's wooden mouse to play with.

"You can't do that!" exclaimed Nick. "You're

biting it, it is my mouse!" He clapped his hands and tried to scare the kittens off. The bells on the puppet clanged and made a noise, which didn't help when Nick tried to get closer to his mouse. The kittens held on to the toy as if it was a real mouse. When Nick pulled the string, the kitten jumped on it from behind. The smallest kitten ran so fast it could catch anything.

"What's your wooden mouse doing here, anyway?" Peter asked.

"It fell out of the window," Nick replied.

"And why didn't you take it back right away?"

Nick did not answer. He was too lazy to run down the stairs and up again to get his mouse.

"Now come on!" said Peter, "or we'll be the last ones to get to playschool."

Many of the children were already at school.

When all the children had arrived, the teacher gave out a large sheet of paper to each one. They could paint whatever they wanted. Nick painted snails. Sarah painted a butterfly. And what did Peter paint? Where did he suddenly get the kitten from?

"Stay in the desk and don't scratch me! Aoo!"
Peter whispered. He had trouble closing the lid
of his desk. He hoped teacher wouldn't notice!

During the next lesson, they had to say the
letters of the alphabet. Nick was allowed to play
at teacher. He pointed the stick to the board,
but he couldn't remember the letter in the square.

54

Paul and Fiona knew what it was. And so did Peter. But Sarah wondered what letter it was too. Do you know it? And do you know the other letters too?

After the morning break, they learned about animals. Several large cards with pictures of different animals were put on the board. Peter was allowed to choose an animal picture and to tell the class everything he knew about it.

Teacher asked, "What is the animal you're pointing to, Peter?"

Several children put up their hands because they knew the answer.

"It's a hedgehog," said Peter.

"And where do hedgehogs live?" asked teacher.

"Here!" cried out the little boy holding his Teddy in his arms, "Here are two of them running!"

"Psst!" whispered the girl next to him. "You mustn't tell!"

But Peter knew the answer, anyway. He said, "The hedgehog lives in the bushes, or in places with dry leaves. When he's hungry, he comes out and eats worms, caterpillars and small mice. He also likes snakes, and if he finds a bird's nest on the ground, he gnaws at the shells of the eggs and sucks them out."

"That's not nice at all!" said the little girl with the red ribbon in her hair. Then she quickly put

her hand in front of her mouth—because only
Peter was supposed to talk about this animal.

"What else do you know about the hedgehogs?" teacher asked.

"I know that it eats apples, too," answered
Peter. "When the fruit falls off the trees in the
autumn, it goes in the gardens and you can hear
it eating before you can even see it." They all

laughed.

"Well done, Peter," said teacher.

After they had all talked about animals, a very large clock was put on the board. "Who knows what time it is?"

"I do!" said Sarah. "It's three o'clock."

"Correct!" said teacher.

"And what time is it when both hands are at

the top?"

"Then it's twelve o'clock!" said Nick.

"Quite right," said the teacher.

Before the bell rings for lunch time, the children usually sing a song.

"What song shall we sing?" asked teacher.

The children all called out, "Three Blind Mice," and the sound of their loud and happy voices

could be heard all over the school.

After lunch the teachers told the children a story. It was all about a pretty little house with an apple tree and flowers in the garden. There was a fence all round the house, where a bird sat and sang songs all day.

On the farm

Mummy asked Sarah, Nick and Peter, "Please go to farmer Browntree over there, and get some

milk and some eggs. But don't hang about!"

Nick didn't want to go at all. "But we've got two hens," he said, "and they lay eggs, too. We've still got some left. And there are three milk bottles in the fridge. I've seen them."

"But the milk from the farm is fresher," said Peter to make Nick come along. Peter preferred the farmer's milk to the one the milkman sold.

Sarah added, "And we only get one egg a day from the two hens. That's not enough for all of us. Besides, Mummy wants to bake a cake, and this evening we're having rice pudding." Nick still wasn't convinced.

"The fat hen laid eight eggs the other day," he said, "I saw them, but Mummy didn't take them. Now they've turned into chicks, and there's already another eight eggs in the nest and no one dares to take them."

"That's right!" Sarah said. "That's so we can have so many chickens next year that we won't need to buy them at the farm any more."

"Ah, well," said Nick. "Alright, I'll come with you. But I want to take Teddy with me."

"O.K.!" said Peter. "You can also carry the egg basket and put Teddy in it whilst it's empty."

Nick quietly trotted behind his brother and sister. Sarah thought he might go back. So Peter stretched out a finger for Nick to hold on to.

"Come on!" said Peter. "If we don't hang about, we'll get to the farm in time to take the eggs from the nest."

"Oh, fine!" Nick cried out. And he ran and jumped so that he would get there first.

On the way they passed by the cows in the meadow. One of the cows had a small calf.

Sarah, Nick and Peter climbed over the fence to look at the calf more closely. They would have

loved to stroke it. But it kept on moving about. "Give it some grass," Sarah suggested to Peter, "perhaps it'll stand still."

A little further on, they discovered that the brown duck had hatched her eggs, and was leading ten little chicks to the pond. They were paddling away with their small webbed-feet and stretching out their beaks to catch mosquitoes.

The smallest duckling, though, sat by the mother duck and didn't want to go in the water. "I'd like to know what they're talking about," said Peter.

The three walked on. In the next meadow they saw some sheep with tiny lambs. The lambs looked so sweet and cuddly.

"I wonder how old this one is?" asked Sarah,

holding a tiny lamb and stroking it.

Peter said, "Five days old, perhaps. But this one is even smaller." Then suddenly they heard pigs grunting. They were running out of the pig-sty so fast that the fattest one stepped on Nick's feet. He pushed Nick so hard that he had trouble stopping himself from falling. At the same time, the pig puffed and squealed but it was as clean as if it was made of marzipan.

"Why do we call them pigs, anyway?" Sarah asked. "They're not at all dirty!" They all laughed.

Peter reminded them, "Do you remember what Mummy said, we are not to hang about? If we don't hurry up now, it'll be dark by the time we get back home." They walked round several sheds and stables and, at last, they found the farmer.

"You've come just at the right time!" said the farmer. "Will you come with me to collect the eggs?"

In the hen house there are four storeys. Nick was allowed to take out the eggs from the bottom shelf. Sarah and Peter took them from the middle. The farmer looked after the top row.

"Marvellous!" he said. "I don't have to stoop down today."

There were so many eggs that the children couldn't count them all. There were brown and white ones, large, thin and small ones. Nick found a nest where a hen was still sitting. It shook its head, all excited, and stretched its neck. Suddenly it stood up and began to cackle very loudly. It then stepped off the hay and ran off.

"It's laid an egg!" Nick called out. As he took the egg in his hand, it was still quite warm.

Sarah said, "There's another hen still sitting here."

"Then we mustn't disturb it!" said the farmer.

When all the nests were emptied, the farmer went outside with the children and filled up their small can with fresh cow's milk. He then gave Sarah two more eggs from his large basket, making sure that Sarah's basket was quite full.

The farmer asked, "What are your two hens doing, then?"

"They've already got eight chicks," answered Sarah, "and next week we'll have eight more."

"Ah!" said the farmer, laughing, "Soon I can buy my eggs from your place."

When Sarah, Nick and Peter returned home, their evening meal was already on the table.

Daddy and Mummy asked, "Where were you for so long?"

"At the farm," replied Peter. "And we didn't really dawdle. We only fed the calf, looked at the ducks, counted the sheep and took out the eggs from the nests."

By the seaside

When the long summer holidays began, the children asked the same question, "Where are we going?"

When Daddy said, "We'll go to the seaside!" they all shouted "Hurray!" and were very excited.

Sarah, Nick and Peter were sitting in the train. They looked through the window as the world flew past and telegraph poles whizzed by. The three children closed their eyes. As their coach swayed on the railway lines, they imagined they were on a ship sailing through the waves.

While the three children were playing with their games, Daddy and Mummy read books. Peter remarked on how the sky was so blue all of a sudden. He had a quick glance, then he shouted, "Look outside!"

The train driver put on the brakes. Sarah and Nick couldn't believe that they were really at the seaside.

On the top of a hill, right by the beach there were two houses. Sarah, Nick and Peter were staying in one with their Mummy and Daddy. They had hardly arrived before they ran barefoot down the slope of the hill, to have a look at the boats. One of the boats had a sail with the picture of a snail on it, and a number 3.

Nick said, "That little boat must be for us. Come on, let's get in it!"

Peter and Sarah thought this was a good idea. Then they realised they didn't know very much about sailing.

"Can it overturn?" asked Nick.

"Yes, of course," Peter said. "If you rock about too much, all boats overturn."

"I can swim," Sarah said. "It's alright for me. If we overturn, I'll just jump into the water."

"But your doll can't swim," Peter said.

"Nor can Teddy," said Nick.

They all agreed that they'd rather not go in the boat without Daddy and Mummy being with them. So they tied up the boat again and left their toys in it. They wanted to have a quick look around. There were a lot of things which they had never seen before.

"There's the fishing harbour over there," said Peter. "Shall we go over there?"

"Oh, yes," said Nick, "I'd like to see real fishing hooks and a real fishing net."

"Do you think that crabs crawl around here?" Sarah asked. "I've got no shoes on ..."

"We're all barefooted," said Peter. "Let's see who gets pinched first."

As they got nearer the fishing harbour, the three of them held their noses. It smelt of fish and fish oil. But they soon got used to the smell, and they were amazed at the number of different kinds of fish which lay in baskets, boxes and nets. Many were mixed with lumps of ice. Others were still moving about and swimming in water, because they were to be sold alive.

There was also a big crab in a net. "How can you eat the crab's hard shell?" asked Nick.

"You don't eat the shell," answered Peter, "Mummy takes the crabmeat out of the shell and the big claws. It's just the meat that we have for tea, Nick."

"Oh! I feel hungry now," said Sarah.

"What are these on top of the crab's shell?" asked Sarah.

Peter answered, "Those are small barnacles; they live on the crab and it can't get rid of them,

even if it sometimes gets cross with them."

"Do you think it's still alive?" Sarah asked. "Can't it come out of the net?"

"Why don't you ask him," said Nick.

"That's not nice of you," Sarah replied. "Besides, his pincers are so big that he could send you both packing in one go!"

Sarah, Nick and Peter had seen enough of the fishing harbour. In the meantime, Daddy and Mummy had come down to the beach with the swimming things and everyone wanted to have a dip in the sea. Peter teased a little girl riding on an inflatable duck. He wanted to have a go on the floating duck.

"What's your name?" asked Peter.

"My name's Gaby." she answered.

"Can you swim?"

"Yes, of course!" Gaby said. Peter paddled along behind the duck. Gaby enjoyed going for a ride. Sarah held on tight to her inflatable fish. She pulled Nick's boat along behind her.

Nick could swim properly, he put on the arm bands for fun; but also so that he wouldn't sink if a wave came over his head. He also had a hand free to wave, and the other hand to pinch his nose.

While Sarah was playing with Nick's boat, she landed back on the beach, without doing anything. Nick did too, he let himself be carried by the waves and soon found himself lying on the

sand again.

When he stood up and looked around him,
the beach seemed smaller than it was before and
the wicker beach chair was nearer the water's
edge.

"Daddy!" shouted Nick. "Where's all the sand
gone?"

Daddy replied, "The water has risen and the

tide has come in."

"And what's that?" asked Peter, who found himself being pushed onto the shore by the waves.

"Why don't you all come here!" said Daddy. "I'll try to explain it to you. All along the coasts, the water gets drawn back every six hours, and then it takes another six hours for the water to return. When the tide goes out, it is called an ebb-tide. When the tide comes in, it is the flow-tide."

"And why does it happen?" Peter asked.

Daddy continued, "The moon and the sun cause this. When you are older and go to school, you'll learn all about it and understand it better. But there's one thing anyone who bathes in the sea must remember. When the tide is going out you mustn't go far out in the water, otherwise you can be pulled out to sea by the waves. It's the same for small boats too."

"Now I know why we floated in to the beach, like pieces of wood," said Nick. "At flow-tide, it is the other way round to the ebb-tide? Is that

right?"

"Quite right," said Daddy, "and now put some dry clothes on, and let's fly the kites. There are apples, lemonade and bars of chocolate in the basket."

Sarah, Nick and Peter stayed on for another four weeks at the seaside. Every day they discovered new things and had different experiences. They even learned how to make a kite, and a small boat for Teddy. They made the masts out of sticks, and they were allowed to cut up a handkerchief for the sails. They want to come back next year.

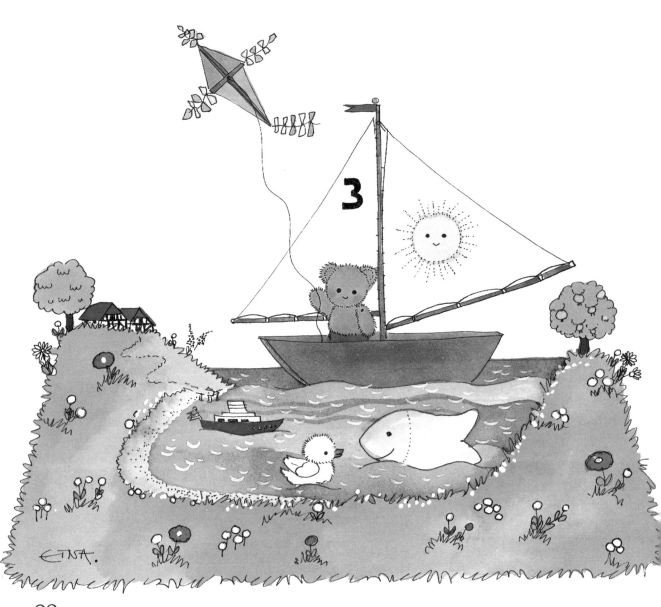

A trip to the mountains

Sarah, Nick and Peter went for an excursion to the mountains. They packed their backpacks with all they needed for the trip. They tramped in Indian file over the hilly meadows and sang songs as they went.

They had a rest on the edge of a footpath and ate the sandwiches, the apples and the boiled eggs. "Oh look," said Nick. "I can see a cable

railway over there. Shall we ask if we can go on it?"

"Yes, great!" shouted Sarah and Peter.

They hurried and put their rucksacks on again. The driver of the cable railway allowed the three children in the passenger cabin. The cabin is so high up above the valley that, the children could see for miles around. Peter got his binoculars out of his backpacks.

"I can see the Mountain Ghost," he said, "he's sitting on the top of a pine tree and licking a choc ice." Sarah and Nick didn't believe him.

When they got to the top, they climbed out of the cabin and Sarah shouted, "It looks just the same here as it did down below. Only the sun's hotter."

"Yes, but I wonder why?" asked Nick.

"Because we are nearer the sun," Peter answered. "And why are there large rocks all over the place?"

"Because the Mountain Ghost plays football here!" Peter told them. They all laughed.

There were steep hills with pine trees and winding meadows, with lots of cows and sheep.

All the animals had bells on their collars, and when they moved about the bells rang loud and clear.

"I bet I know why the farmers put bells on the cattle." Nick said.

"Go on, tell us then!" shouted the others.

"So that they can be found if they wander off and get lost."

Sarah listened and said, "I think I can already hear one that's got lost." She went to the slope and the others followed her. And sure enough there was a small sheep on a patch of grass, eating flowers.

"Now why did it wander off down there, are the flowers down there tastier than up here?"

"Let's see if we can chase it back up here again," Peter said.

They took off their backpacks and climbed down the slope. It was not very easy to make the sheep come up again. Sarah picked some fresh grass and held it in her hand.

Nick and Peter made sure it didn't turn back. The little sheep saw the rest of the flock in the distance and it leapt off, jumping over shrubs and tufts of grass.

"What if we hadn't been here ... !" said Peter.

They opened their backpacks and took out the drawing paper and colouring pens. They looked for a nice spot in the meadow where they could draw. Sarah drew a little sheep like the one they had just saved. Then she drew flowers and ladybirds. Peter wanted to draw a mountain deer, but a butterfly landed on his piece of paper, so he changed his mind.

"You forgot something here," Sarah told him, and she drew a line in for Peter.

Nick drew a cow, one with its tongue out, and then another one that looked as if it was staring. He discovered that he hadn't got the right colour to put in some grass for the meadow.

"Have you got a green colouring pen, Peter?" Nick asked.

"No, we haven't got any," replied Peter. "Make it yourself!"

"Make it myself? What d'you mean?" called out Nick.

Peter said, "Use some yellow. Colour everything in yellow then go over it with some blue!"
Nick tried it on a corner of his piece of paper.
Peter was quite right.

Nick tried some other colours to see which could be mixed together, and he discovered that: yellow and blue make green; yellow and red make orange; blue and red make violet; green and red make brown.

"How can you make red if you haven't got it?" asked Nick.

"You must have red," answered Peter. "Also blue and yellow. That's all you need to make up any colour."

The sun was shining so strongly that Peter was getting too warm. "Come on," he said, "let's put our shorts on, they're in the backpacks, and let's run around barefoot!"

They all agreed. They put away their colouring things carefully and ran off to a tiny lake, where they paddled for a while.

Sarah, Nick and Peter saw some small ducks. The ducks were used to being given some titbits by anyone walking around the shore of the lake.

"Have you got any bread left, Peter?" asked Sarah.

"No," replied Peter, "but we've still got the biscuits and chocolate."

Sarah, Nick and Peter suddenly realised they were hungry. They walked over to the shore and unpacked the food that was still left. The ducks

waddled along when they saw the children tearing off paper packets, they came out of the water and said, "Quaack-quaack."

"Yes, you'll get something," Peter said to a duck in front of him with its neck out to see what was inside the paper. It then opened its beak so wide that Peter gave it a whole biscuit in one go. When the duck closed its beak, the biscuit stuck out. It swallowed and swallowed, but the biscuit was too big for its throat. Then the duck ran to the water, dipped the biscuit in and as it was wet and soft, the duck swallowed the biscuit like mash. "She's crafty," said Peter.

The other ducks did the same with the hard biscuits. Sarah, Nick and Peter threw them bits into the water and watched the ducks fighting over each piece. The children didn't notice how quickly their biscuits were disappearing. They only had chocolate and sweets left. But ducks don't like sweets and chocolate, so Sarah, Nick and Peter ate the sweets. Then they took off their wet clothes, dried themselves and put on their walking clothes again.

"I can see a house with bells on it," called out Nick. "Let's go there."

"Yes, fine!" said Peter. "Now we've got a new spot to aim for!"

The way to the house was very steep, and the children had to keep stopping to have a rest and take off their heavy backpacks. Suddenly Peter jumped up, skipped around and shouted, "Ooa-Ooa-Ooa!" He shook his arms and legs. Nick

and Sarah laughed. They thought Peter must
have seen the Mountain Ghost. Then they
noticed that they were sitting in the middle of
an anthill. The little ants were very frightened
too, because their home was smashed up. They
rushed to and fro, very excitedly.

Luckily, the house with all the bells on it was
quite near, and Sarah, Nick and Peter were

pleased they made the effort. The house was a small mountain restaurant. There were sausages and chips and beans, and fresh milk from the cows. They even had ice-cream. The three children looked in their purses to see how much money they had between them. Luckily they had enough. Even their toys could eat with them, the rabbit, Teddy bear and the doll.

Peter asked the waitress, "Why are there stones on the roof?"

"That's so that the storm doesn't blow the roof off," she answered.

As it was such a hot day it was difficult to imagine that the wind could be so strong. The children then realized that it was time they went home. They had great fun running down the hills. They ran so fast that sometimes they began to slide down. Sarah, Nick and Peter thought this very funny and were very happy as they arrived safely home.

A visit to Uncle Bill

One dark and rainy day, Sarah, Nick and Peter found the large album of photographs in a cupboard.

"That's me!" shouted Nick when he saw the picture of a boy wearing red trousers and feeding a little horse with an apple. "And that's me again!"

Teasing her younger brother, Sarah said, "You were a nice little boy then!"

"Whose are the three little horses?" Peter wanted to know.

"They're mine!" Nick replied. "That was at

Uncle Bill's, and he got them all out of the stable for me."

"Didn't you help at all?"

"Of course I did," said Nick. "I washed and brushed them down, when they were outside. There was a hundred years of dust on them. The rocking horse used to belong to Grandma, and the one with the small wheels was Grandpa's. Uncle Bill had the hobby horse when he was a little boy. I couldn't ride them right away, I had to wait until they were quite dry again."

"Aren't they made of wood?" asked Sarah.

"Only inside," said Nick. "But they're covered in material, and when they were wet they were sticky."

"That sounds fun!" Peter said. "Tell us what else happened at Uncle Bill's! Are there ghosts in his old house?"

"It was summer and the evenings were lovely and warm. Auntie Dot had cooked a delicious supper which we were all enjoying, when all of a sudden there was a terrible commotion up-stairs. Uncle Bill picked up a large stick and rushed upstairs to see who was there. Auntie Dot and I sat very still while we waited to find out who it was. For a long time it was very quiet and I wanted to see if Uncle Bill needed any help. He came downstairs looking very puzzled. There was no one there. The next evening we were playing 'Snap' and having lots of fun shouting and laughing, when the noise upstairs started.

We looked at each other and, again Uncle Bill picked up a stick and rushed upstairs. But, once again, no one was there, and the noise stopped immediately. This went on for a whole week. Then one evening when the noise started Uncle Bill picked up his stick and crept quietly upstairs. He peeped into the room where he thought the noise came from. There on the windowsill was a beautiful mummy squirrel. Her baby squirrels were leaping about and jumping from the bedposts to the top of the wardrobe and onto the dressing table. They were having a lot of fun and making very alarming noises. They had seen the window open and decided it would be nice and safe to learn to jump.

Uncle Bill crept downstairs again and told us
what he had seen. Then he pretended to rush
upstairs – the squirrels scampered away. We all
laughed because we had been so frightened by
the noises and it was only a squirrel family enjoying themselves."

Peter asked him, "Have you got a story like that for each one of the photographs?"

Nick carried on, "See if you can guess who this is? It isn't me! That's Grandpa, 80 years ago!" They were all astonished.

"But this is you!" Sarah shouted.

"That's right," Nick replied. "I wanted to try out Uncle Bill's hobby horse, and I rode into town with it. It's really useful. It hoots when you sit on it."

"And if you're tired, you just put it under your arm and walk on. Then you've got both hands free and you can put one in your pocket, and eat an ice cream with the other one."

As Sarah turned the pages of the album, she cried out, "Oh, look here! There's Nick on Grandma's rocking horse!"

Peter asked, "What about the armour and sword, are they Grandpa's?"

"No," said Nick, "I made them myself."

"Out of what?", Peter asked him.

"Out of cardboard," Nick answered. "It wasn't easy at all, because the cardboard was very thick. Uncle Bill helped me to cut out the armour. I only had a pair of scissors."

Peter said, "I'd like to have the sword. It looks real, even if it's made out of paper. But where did you get the handle?"

"Made it by myself as well," Nick answered. "I simply sawed two pieces of wood, then I made a point on one piece, made a hole in the other and stuck them both together. Then I stuck the cardboard blade in it."

Sarah asked, "Did you also make the small train at the back?"

"Yes," Nick answered. "But it was printed on a piece of card; I painted it, and cut it out, then stuck the finished pieces together. If you look closely, you'll see that the wheels don't turn round."

"You had a nice little corner at Uncle Bill's and Auntie Dot's," Sarah said as she was looking at the next photograph. "Does that board with the alphabet on it always hang on the wall? Or did they put it there specially for you?"

"That used to be Uncle Bill's playroom," Nick said, "and they left it so that the children who visit them have a room where they can romp around. Uncle Bill painted the alphabet when he was my age. And the picture of the house too. He was given the puppet once as a birthday present. The bricks are made of wood, and the marbles on the floor are not glass ones, but they're made of clay, and they're not very round because Uncle Bill made them himself."

Sarah said, "Turn back a page, please! Isn't that a hamster, sitting in a cage?"

Nick laughed, "You fell for it! It's a mouse made out of material, Auntie Dot made it out of a stocking. The only real thing is the apple on the window seat."

"But the drum is real, too!" Peter called out. "I bet it's made of tin, and that Uncle Bill made as much noise with it as you did when you banged on it?"

"You're quite right!" Nick said.

"But that's our rocking horse," Peter said. "How did it get in Uncle Bill's garden?"

"I think you're a bit confused!" Sarah said.

"This plum tree's in our garden. Don't you recognise the long branch we swing on?"

Sarah and her dolls

When Sarah saw the photograph of the little girl with the doll, she shouted, "That's not me!"

Peter teased her, "I don't think you've changed much, Sarah!"

Sarah could remember when this photograph was taken. It was just after her birthday and she had been given a beautiful doll. She had a party and invited all her little friends. They played games and wore party hats, and had a lovely tea. When her friends had gone home, her Mummy and Daddy gave her the doll. Grandma and Grandad gave Sarah a doll's pram, and Peter gave her the book which she was reading to her doll in the photograph. It was a lovely day and the photograph brought back lots of happy memories.

The next photograph showed Sarah sitting in her bedroom on the floor with her doll. The kitten was also trying to play and kept tapping the doll's foot.

"But tell me, Sarah," Peter asked while he looked at the photograph of her room, "is there still something inside the box of sweets up there on the shelf?"

"You can go into my room and look for your-

self," Sarah answered. "But if the box isn't empty, close it again and bring it here!"

Peter rushed up the stairs to look for the box.

"This is a good photograph of your doll having her lunch."

"She was three years old," Sarah said. "I used

to make some pretend lunch for her. Mummy would let me put some cereal in a bowl and I mixed it up with milk so that it looked like baby food. The kitten liked to eat it up when I had finished playing, so it wasn't wasted."

Sarah remembered that she had to wear a little apron when she was playing at cooking. She tried not to spill too much food on herself.

"I can remember that she could walk the first day you had her," Nick said. "You got it for your birthday and she marched straight into my Indian fort like a robot."

"Well, she's got a motor in her stomach and when I wind her up she walks straight on without looking, just like you. You knocked over a large vase, anyway!"

Nick laughed, "Why does she cry out, 'Mama'?"

"She wants something!" Sarah answered. "She learnt that from you!"

"In this picture," Nick said, "our kitten, Sally, looks as if she's scared of fish. Was it dead?"

Sarah laughed, "No, silly, the fish was made

of cardboard, it came from our fishing game."

As they turned over the pages, Sarah was overjoyed when they came to the photograph of the doll in the pram. "That was on my birthday too!" she shouted. "I still remember it well.

Grandma and Grandad gave me the doll's pram."

Sarah hadn't noticed that Peter was sitting next to her holding the box of sweets between his knees. His mouth was so full of fruit gums that he didn't dare open it.

Sarah looked at her doll and shouted, "You're so pretty I could eat you!"

Peter couldn't help laughing, and as he did, half the fruit gums flew out of his mouth and fell onto the photograph album.

A yellow gum got stuck on the photograph, right between the doll's hands. It all happened so quickly and it looked so funny and they laughed so loud that Mummy came in to see what was going on.

The children couldn't speak as they were laughing so much and when Mummy looked at the sweet she began to laugh too.

"It was an accident," Peter said with his hand in front of his mouth so that he wouldn't lose any more sweets.

"Yes, yes, I know!" said Mummy.

Then she took the photograph out of the album and went to the kitchen to clean it up.

Mummy also took away the box of sweets from Peter. When Sarah turned to the next page, Peter burst out laughing again.

"What's so funny now?" Nick asked.

"Just look at Teddy," Peter said, pointing to the bear and the little boy with the blue shorts.

"Is that you?" Nick asked.

"Yes, it is," Peter replied. "Don't you recognise me."

"No," Sarah said. "Since when did you play with girls?"

"Boys or girls, it's all the same, main thing it's fun." Peter replied. "The girls were playing with their dolls and laughing, so, I remember, I took my teddybear out to join them in the garden. You can see two of Sarah's dolls sitting on the swing. We played in the garden all afternoon as it was such warm and sunny weather. You can also see the lovely rosy red apples in the trees, and lots of flowers in the garden."

Sarah remembered that afternoon, too. They really enjoyed looking at the photographs and remembering happy times like those.

"And where am I?" asked Nick.

Sarah answered, "On that day you were in bed with chicken pox. And we all caught it from

you. And on the same evening, we went out to have a sack race but the sack had had some coal in it, and I had to stay in the bath for three hours afterwards to get clean."

"That's a nice photograph of you," Peter said. "Did Mummy take it?"

"Yes," Sarah answered. "I had lots of fun putting my doll to bed and making sure she was

comfortable."

"Oh!" Sarah called out, "that's Susie again, quite alone! Isn't she cute?"

"Yes, she is!" Nick said. "But just after you

117

took that photograph of her she fell over!"
   "How d'you know that, then?" asked Sarah.
   "Because the cat moved out of the way as soon as the camera had clicked!" laughed Peter.

Peter at the party

"Toot-toot! That's me!" shouted Peter.

"When was that, then?" Nick asked.

"One Easter time," Peter answered. "I remember I received a small duck and I put it on the car radiator; I stuck another one on the door.

Then after that, I came first in the soap box race."

"And what prize did you get?" Sarah asked him. "I won a teddy bear."

Nick wanted to know how old Peter was then.

"I don't know," replied Peter. "But I remember that I had a small brother who was just learning to walk, and that was you!"

"So I was smaller than your teddy, then?" Nick said, laughing. "I hope you took me for a drive in your car too."

"I did try," Peter said, "but you started to cry. You see, it was a pedal car and when I put you on my knees you kept on jumping up and down and I didn't like that."

They all laughed and Nick was not cross with his big brother because he hadn't taken him for a ride. Peter had to pedal hard in the toy train just like in the pedal car. "Where are those toys now?" Sarah asked.

Peter answered, "The soap box is the same one we have now, only it has had a couple of new parts added to it. But the train is broken."

"Couldn't the engine be mended any more?"
Peter was embarrassed. "No," he answered,
"It was only made of light wood and I left it out
in the rain too long. One day, as I sat on it, it
broke up under me."
Looking at another photograph Sarah called

out, "Oh, how sweet! There's my big brother fishing! Where was this, then?"

"Don't know," said Peter. "I only remember that later on, I really did catch a fish on the hook.

Then I threw it back in the water."

"And in this photograph where are you going to?"

Peter replied, "It was somebody's birthday, and I was invited."

"Can you still remember what present you took with you?"

"I took a small bag with figures and animals made out of wood. It's in my shoulder bag."

"Are they the ones in this photograph?" Nick asked.

"Yes," Peter replied. "We played with them in the sand. They were so nice I'd rather have kept them. Daddy gave me some later on because I liked them so much."

"Who are the three children running there?" Sarah wanted to know.

"I can't remember that!" Peter answered. "They were probably invited to the birthday party. I remember one thing though. When the cake arrived we played a game called Peter and Paul. We were all given the name either Peter or Paul and when my friend's Mummy called out 'Peter' all the Peters were allowed to eat. Then she called out 'Paul' and all the Pauls ate some cake and the Peters had to stop. If you were caught eating when you shouldn't have been, you had to pay a fine. I had to pay a fine, then. For

example, a shoe or both shoes, or everything in your trouser pockets!" Peter laughed. "The cherry cake tasted so good that, to finish, I had to sit barefoot at table."

Nick said, "We'll play that on my birthday

as well! And when the party was over, did you have a go on the slide?"

"As you can see, we did," said Peter. "But the slide was much too short, which was a pity. As soon as you sat at the top, it didn't take long to get to the bottom and had to wait for your turn again."

"A slide's great!" said Nick. "Wish I had one like that."

"I think it's too short," Sarah said. "Besides, how could you get your head under the bar at the top?"

"You're right," answered Peter, "it looks quite a small opening from here, but really it was quite wide enough."

Nick wanted to know, "Did you play any other games?"

"Yes," Peter answered, "I remember another one. There was an enormous bowl full of different coloured sweets. One person was sent out of the room and the children left in the room agreed on one colour of sweet. They called the one outside back in, and he had to pick out the

colour he thought had been chosen. If he was
wrong he could keep the sweet. He carried on
until he had chosen the right colour. Then it was
someone else's turn."

"That's a really good game!" Nick called out.
"We'll play that on my birthday too!"

"I'd rather play it right now," Sarah suggested. "And we'll play it a second time on Nick's birthday!"

Peter sighed, "Sarah, your box of sweets is almost empty ... !"

"What a shame," Sarah said, "then we'll have to wait for Nick's birthday. Tell us what else you did."

"We played at cutting the chocolate. You get a wooden plate and a knife and fork, and have to unwrap a chocolate with them and then cut it and eat it. You throw dice for your turn and when you get a 6 it's your turn. It's great fun and you get some chocolate too!"

Peter could remember that party very well. He carried on with his story, "It was the first birthday party I had been invited to. I didn't know what to expect but it certainly was fun and we all had lots of good things to eat. I made some new friends at the party and I still see one or two of them sometimes. I know that one boy goes to our playschool as well."

Nick was looking at another photograph.

"Look how you're sitting on that swing!"

"Yes, it does look funny," Peter agreed. "I took my teddybear with me all the time. I was waving to the other children because mummy had come to take me home."

As they turned over the pages, Peter dis-

covered a picture of his teddybear which he had never seen before. Sarah blushed. "Did you take that picture, Sarah?" Peter asked her.

"Yes I did," said Sarah. "I used your camera when you weren't looking!"

"That will cost you three fruit gums from your sweet box!"

"Alright!" answered Sarah, "if you can find any in the box!"

The Punch and Judy show

"Shall we have a Punch and Judy show?" Sarah suggested. I don't fancy looking at photographs any more."

"I don't either!" Peter said. "But where are our puppets?"

"I've got the puppets," Nick said, "but I think it's boring if only three of us play. Then there's only one of us left to watch the show. That's no fun."

Sarah said, "We can go over to the Matthews' house and ask Lucy and Richard to come. They'll be at home now."

"Yes, good idea! You go and ask them," Peter said. "And while you go, I'll get the show ready and Nick can get the puppets."

Nick and Peter ran upstairs to their room and Sarah put the photograph album back in the cupboard. Then she went to the neighbours house. Lucy and Richard were allowed to come. All children love a Punch and Judy show.

When Sarah came back, Peter and Nick had already set up the Punch and Judy stage in the hallway, and put a long bench for the audience to sit on. The curtain was still closed, but Nick and Peter were making noises and giggling behind the scenes.

Sarah whispered, "I wonder what they've thought up?"

Suddenly, all was quiet and the curtain

opened. A little bell tinkled. Then a red pointed cap popped up, and Punch was there.

"Good morning, dear children! Tra-la-la!" he called out. "Have you seen Judy?"

"Here she comes!" shouted Lucy and Richard.

Then, two little eyes and a pair of rabbit's ears popped up, and they all began to laugh loudly.

"What are you laughing at?" asked Punch.

Sarah was just about to say, "At the rabbit!" but he had already disappeared.

"A rabbit's just been looking at us!" Lucy called out. "But he's gone now!"

"Oh, dear!" Punch said. "Judy, come here! If there's a rabbit there, we'll rescue him right away and bring him back to the woods. Because I saw a crocodile there earlier."

They all shouted, "There's the crocodile!"

"Where?" Punch called out, looking all around him.

"It was right there!" said Sarah. "But he's gone again." The show began to get exciting.

"Now be quiet!" said Punch. "Where did you say the crocodile was?"

"There!" they all shouted, pointing to the right.
But as Punch and Judy moved off to the right
of the stage, the crocodile suddenly appeared

from the left corner.

"There it is, there!" the children shouted. And then they shouted even louder, "There's the rabbit again!"

Punch and Judy whizzed left and right across the stage. Sarah bent over with laughter.

There! All of a sudden they all heard a loud clatter of teeth, the crocodile had caught the rabbit. It did look awful. Richard started to cry and Lucy comforted him. But Sarah kept on laughing.

"Aaah!" cried out Punch, "got you at last!" and he opened the crocodile's jaws and rescued the rabbit. Judy pulled the rabbit out and stroked it, and Punch made sure that the crocodile didn't run away. But the poor rabbit put both its paws in front of its eyes, and cried so pitifully.

Judy asked the rabbit, "Are you hurt?"

"No," the rabbit answered, and cried even more.

"So, what's the matter, then?" Sarah asked. "Tell us what it is!"

The poor rabbit cried out, "Crocodile's taken

away my lettuce leaf!'' and it cried even more.
Punch was very relieved, and said, "Oh, well,

137

if that's all I'll send Judy to the kitchen right now. She'll get a whole lettuce for you to eat."

The rabbit laughed again. And Lucy, Richard and Sarah were happy too especially when the policeman arrived with a cage to lock up the crocodile.

But then, the crocodile started to cry. It groaned, "I promise I didn't want to eat the rabbit. I only wanted the lettuce leaf."

Punch asked the children, "Do you believe the crocodile, do you think he is telling the truth?"

"No!" they shouted.

"Then," said Punch, "the crocodile will have to stay in the cage."

"Hurrah!" shouted Lucy and Richard.

"No!" Sarah cried out. "The policeman should send it back to Africa where it can bathe in the river, where there are no rabbits."

Punch then said, "Mr. Policeman, could you see to it that the crocodile is flown back to its own country, and that it will be well cared for."

"Just as you say!" answered the policeman.

In the meantime, Peter and Nick opened up

another curtain and there were five other rabbits there.

"Hurrah!" shouted the children.

Then they called out, "Punch, Punch, the king's coming!"

The king said, "Dear Punch, dear Judy, I have

140

come to give you a reward because I saw that
you let the crocodile go free again."

Sarah whispered, "There's another crocodile!"

There was another crocodile there, but it was the one that lives under Peter's bed! He doesn't eat rabbits, he is friendly. But he just wanted to say hello to the children and join in the fun.